ENGERS.

ALL OURSELVES

E A TEAM.

MIGHTIEST.

YPE THING.

—TONY STARK, *THE AVENGERS*

YOU NEED US. YES, THE WORLD IS A VULNERABLE PLACE, AND YES, WE HELP MAKE IT THAT WAY, BUT WE'RE ALSO THE ONES BEST QUALIFIED TO DEFEND IT.

—BLACK WIDOW, *CAPTAIN AMERICA: THE WINTER SOLDIER*

PART OF A BIGGER UNIVERSE

UNFORGETTABLE QUOTES FROM THE MARVEL CINEMATIC UNIVERSE

Compiled by Steve Behling

LOS ANGELES • NEW YORK

"You think you're the only Super Hero in the world? Mr. Stark, you've become part of a bigger universe. You just don't know it yet."

—Nick Fury, *Iron Man*

TRY TO KEEP UP.

—CAPTAIN MARVEL, *CAPTAIN MARVEL*

"Oh, I make grave mistakes all the time. Everything seems to work out."

—Thor, *Thor: Ragnarok*

WHOSOEVER HOLDS THIS HAMMER, IF HE BE WORTHY, SHALL POSSESS THE POWER OF THOR.

—ODIN, *THOR*

STAR-LORD: I'm gonna ask you this
one time: Where is Gamora?

IRON MAN: Yeah, I'll do you one better.
Who is Gamora?

DRAX: I'll do *you* one better.
Why is Gamora?

—*AVENGERS: INFINITY WAR*

"I'm gonna die

surrounded

by the biggest

idiots

in the galaxy."

—Gamora, *Guardians of the Galaxy*

—GROOT,
GUARDIANS OF
THE GALAXY

"Your ancestors

  called it magic,

  and you

  call it science.

  Well, I come

  from a place

  where they

  are one

  and the same."

—Thor, *Thor*

I REALLY MISS THE DAYS WHEN THE WEIRDEST THING SCIENCE EVER CREATED WAS ME.

—STEVE ROGERS, *AVENGERS: AGE OF ULTRON*

WE CREATE OUR OWN DEMONS.

—TONY STARK, *IRON MAN 3*

"It hurts,

doesn't it?

Being lied to.

Being told

you're one thing

and then

learning

it's all a fiction."

—Loki, *Thor: Ragnarok*

"I'm made of rocks, as you can see. But don't let that intimidate you. You don't need to be afraid unless you're made of scissors. Just a little rock-paper-scissor joke for you."

—Korg, *Thor: Ragnarok*

AIN'T NO THING LIKE ME, 'CEPT ME!

—ROCKET, *GUARDIANS OF THE GALAXY*

THOR: Wrong!
        Where we have to go is Nidavellir.

DRAX: That's a made-up word.

THOR: All words are made up.

CAROL DANVERS: It's two words. Mar-Vell.

NICK FURY: Mar-Vell. Marvel sounds a lot better.

—*CAPTAIN MARVEL*

KAECILIUS: How long have you been at Kamar-Taj, Mister . . . ?

DOCTOR STRANGE: It's Doctor.

KAECILIUS: Mister Doctor.

DOCTOR STRANGE: It's Strange.

KAECILIUS: Maybe. Who am I to judge?

—*DOCTOR STRANGE*

DUDE. YOU'RE EMBARRASSING ME IN FRONT OF THE WIZARDS.

—TONY STARK, *AVENGERS: INFINITY WAR*

I'M A WARRIOR, AND AN ASSASSIN. I DO NOT DANCE.

—GAMORA, *GUARDIANS OF THE GALAXY*

"There are

two types

of beings

in the universe:

those who dance,

and those

who do not."

—Drax, *Guardians of the Galaxy Vol. 2*

THOR: If you help me get back to Asgard, I can help you get back to Earth.

HULK: Earth hates Hulk.

THOR: Earth loves you! They love you. You're one of the Avengers. One of the team. One of our friends. This is what friends do, they support each other.

HULK: You're Banner's friend.

THOR: I'm not Banner's friend. I prefer you.

HULK: Banner's friend.

THOR: I don't even like Banner.

—*THOR: RAGNAROK*

BRUCE BANNER: Wait, you're just using me to get to the Hulk.

THOR: What? No!

BRUCE BANNER: It's gross. You don't care about me.
You're not my friend.

THOR: No! I don't even like the Hulk. He's all like . . .
"Smash, smash, smash." I prefer you.

BRUCE BANNER: Thanks.

THOR: But if I'm being honest, when it comes to fighting
evil beings, he is very powerful and useful.

BRUCE BANNER: Yeah, Banner's powerful and useful, too.

THOR: Is he, though?

—THOR: RAGNAROK

"I built this for you. And someday you'll realize that it represents a whole lot more than just people's inventions. It represents my life's work. This is the key to the future. I'm limited by the technology of my time, but one day you'll figure this out. And when you do, you will change the world. What is and always will be my greatest creation . . . is you."

—Howard Stark, *Iron Man 2*

TONY STARK: I thought my dad was tough on me. And now, looking back, I just remember the good stuff, you know? He did drop the odd pearl.

HOWARD STARK: Yeah? Like what?

TONY STARK: "No amount of money ever bought a second of time."

HOWARD STARK: Smart guy.

TONY STARK: He did his best.

HOWARD STARK: Let me tell you, that kid's not even here yet, and there's nothing I wouldn't do for him.

—*AVENGERS: ENDGAME*

MY FAITH'S IN PEOPLE, I GUESS. INDIVIDUALS. AND I'M HAPPY TO SAY THAT, FOR THE MOST PART, THEY HAVEN'T LET ME DOWN. WHICH IS WHY I CAN'T LET THEM DOWN EITHER.

—STEVE ROGERS, *CAPTAIN AMERICA: CIVIL WAR*

"Wakanda will no longer watch from the shadows. We cannot. We must not. We will work to be an example of how we, as brothers and sisters on this earth, should treat each other. Now, more than ever, the illusions of division threaten our very existence. We all know the truth: More connects us than separates us. But in times of crisis the wise build bridges, while the foolish build barriers. We must find a way to look after one another, as if we were one single tribe."

—King T'Challa, *Black Panther*

DOCTOR STRANGE: I went forward in time to view alternate futures. To see all the possible outcomes of the coming conflict.

STAR-LORD: How many did you see?

DOCTOR STRANGE: 14,000,605.

IRON MAN: How many did we win?

DOCTOR STRANGE: One.

—AVENGERS: INFINITY WAR

IRON MAN: You said one out of fourteen million, we win, yeah? Tell me this is it.

DOCTOR STRANGE: If I tell you what happens, it won't happen.

IRON MAN: You better be right.

—AVENGERS: ENDGAME

YOU GET TO DECIDE WHAT KIND OF KING YOU ARE GOING TO BE.

—NAKIA, *BLACK PANTHER*

"Bury me in the ocean with my ancestors that jumped from the ships. 'Cause they knew death was better than bondage."

—Killmonger, *Black Panther*

STEVE ROGERS: You ready to follow Captain America into the jaws of death?

BUCKY BARNES: Hell, no! The little guy from Brooklyn who was too dumb not to run away from a fight—I'm following him.

—*CAPTAIN AMERICA: THE FIRST AVENGER*

YOU WERE MEANT FOR MORE THAN THIS, YOU KNOW?

—PEGGY CARTER, *CAPTAIN AMERICA: THE FIRST AVENGER*

VICTORY AT THE EXPENSE OF THE INNOCENT IS NO VICTORY AT ALL.

—KING T'CHAKA, *CAPTAIN AMERICA: CIVIL WAR*

"Everyone fails

at who they're

supposed to be, Thor.

The measure

of a person,

of a hero,

is how well

they succeed at

being who they are."

—Frigga, *Avengers: Endgame*

"Our very strength

invites challenge.

Challenge

incites conflict.

And conflict . . .

breeds

catastrophe."

—Vision, *Captain America: Civil War*

I CAN'T CONTROL THEIR FEAR. ONLY MY OWN.

—WANDA MAXIMOFF, *CAPTAIN AMERICA: CIVIL WAR*

I NEVER FREEZE.

—KING T'CHALLA, *BLACK PANTHER*

SHURI: Did he freeze?

OKOYE: Like an antelope in headlights.

—*BLACK PANTHER*

"It's not a bad thing, finding out that you don't have all the answers. You start asking the right questions."

—Erik Selvig, *Thor*

I AM LOYAL TO THE THRONE. NO MATTER WHO SITS UPON IT. WHAT ARE YOU LOYAL TO?

—OKOYE, *BLACK PANTHER*

YOU LOOK GREAT, CAP. AS FAR AS I'M CONCERNED, THAT'S AMERICA'S ASS.

—ANT-MAN, *AVENGERS: ENDGAME*

PETER QUILL: How the hell is this dude still alive?

DRAX: He is not a dude. *You're* a dude. This . . .
this is a *man*. A handsome, muscular man. . . .
It's like a pirate had a baby with an angel.

GAMORA: It's like his muscles are made of Chitauri metal
fibers. . . .

PETER QUILL: Stop massaging his muscles! Wake him up.

MANTIS: Wake.

THOR: Who the hell are you guys?

—*AVENGERS: INFINITY WAR*

THOR: This is a friend of mine, Tree.

GROOT: I am GROOT!

STEVE ROGERS: I am Steve Rogers.

—AVENGERS: INFINITY WAR

YOU CAN'T BE A "FRIENDLY NEIGHBORHOOD SPIDER-MAN" IF THERE'S NO NEIGHBORHOOD.

—SPIDER-MAN, *AVENGERS: INFINITY WAR*

YOU'RE THE ONE WHO WANTED TO WIN, AND I JUST WANTED A SISTER!

—NEBULA, *GUARDIANS OF THE GALAXY VOL. 2*

YOU WILL ALWAYS BE MY SISTER.

—GAMORA, *GUARDIANS OF THE GALAXY VOL. 2*

"Nidavellir? That place is a legend—they make the most powerful, horrific weapons to ever torment the universe. I would very much like to go there, please."

—Rocket, *Avengers: Infinity War*

JUST BECAUSE SOMETHING WORKS DOESN'T MEAN IT CAN'T BE IMPROVED.

—SHURI, *BLACK PANTHER*

THAT'S MY SECRET, CAP. I'M ALWAYS ANGRY.

—BRUCE BANNER, *THE AVENGERS*

"Hey,

big guy.

Sun's getting

real low."

—Black Widow, *Avengers: Age of Ultron*

"Compromise where you can.

Where you can't, don't.

Even if everyone is telling you

that something wrong

is something right.

Even if the whole world

is telling you to move,

it is your duty to

plant yourself like a tree,

look them in the eye,

and say, 'No, *you* move.'"

—Peggy Carter, *Captain America: Civil War*

FOR AS LONG AS I CAN REMEMBER, I JUST WANTED TO DO WHAT WAS RIGHT.

—STEVE ROGERS, *CAPTAIN AMERICA: THE WINTER SOLDIER*

THAT'S HOW YOU PUNCH.

—HOPE VAN DYNE, *ANT-MAN*

"Hey, Cap, can you hear me? Cap, it's Sam. Can you hear me? On your left."

—Sam Wilson, *Avengers: Endgame*

WENDY LAWSON: Wonderful view, isn't it?

CAROL DANVERS: I prefer the view from up there.

WENDY LAWSON: You'll get there soon enough, Ace.

—*CAPTAIN MARVEL*

THE CITY IS FLYING. WE'RE FIGHTING AN ARMY OF ROBOTS. AND I HAVE A BOW AND ARROW. NONE OF THIS MAKES SENSE.

—HAWKEYE, *AVENGERS: AGE OF ULTRON*

HIGH

FURT

FASTER

HER, HER, HER, BABY.

—CAROL DANVERS, CAPTAIN MARVEL

WE BECAME YOUR REAL FAMILY.

—MONICA RAMBEAU, *CAPTAIN MARVEL*

"You are Carol Danvers. You are the woman on the black box risking her life to do the right thing. My best friend. Who supported me as a mother and a pilot way before anyone else did. You are smart, funny, and a huge pain in the ass. You were the most powerful person I knew, way before you could shoot fire from your fists."

—Maria Rambeau, *Captain Marvel*

"Whatever happens tomorrow, you must promise me one thing. That you will stay who you are. Not a perfect soldier, but a good man."

—Professor Erskine, *Captain America: The First Avenger*

THIS IS THE FIGHT OF OUR LIVES. AND WE'RE GOING TO WIN. WHATEVER IT TAKES.

—STEVE ROGERS, *AVENGERS: ENDGAME*

BIG HERO MOMENT.

—MARIA RAMBEAU, *CAPTAIN MARVEL*

"I shouldn't be alive . . . unless it was for a reason. I'm not crazy, Pepper. I just finally know what I have to do. And I know in my heart that it's right."

—Tony Stark, *Iron Man*

MARIA RAMBEAU:	Call me young lady again, and I'm gonna put my foot where it's not supposed to be.
TALOS:	Am I supposed to guess where that is?
NICK FURY AND CAROL DANVERS:	Your ass.

—CAPTAIN MARVEL

PETER PARKER: Hi. I'm Peter Parker.

CAPTAIN MARVEL: Hey, Peter Parker. You got something for me?

PETER PARKER: I don't know how you're going to get through all that.

SCARLET WITCH: Don't worry.

OKOYE: She's got help.

—*AVENGERS: ENDGAME*

IT'S HARD FOR A GOOD MAN TO BE KING.

—KING T'CHAKA, *BLACK PANTHER*

"A wise

king never

seeks out war.

But he must

always be

ready for it."

—Odin, *Thor*

CAROL DANVERS: You stole me. From my home. From my family. My friends.

SUPREME INTELLIGENCE: It's cute how hard you try. But remember, without us, you're weak. You're flawed. Helpless. We saved you. Without us, you're only human.

CAROL DANVERS: You're right. I'm only human.

SUPREME INTELLIGENCE: On Hala, you were reborn: Vers.

CAROL DANVERS: My name is *Carol*.

—*CAPTAIN MARVEL*

WHEN I WENT UNDER, THE WORLD WAS AT WAR. I WAKE UP, THEY SAY WE WON. THEY DIDN'T SAY WHAT WE LOST.

—STEVE ROGERS, *THE AVENGERS*

AVENGERS, ASSEMBLE.

—CAPTAIN AMERICA, *AVENGERS: ENDGAME*

"When you can do the things that I can, but you don't, and then the bad things happen, they happen because of you."

—Peter Parker, *Captain America: Civil War*

WHAT'S A RACCOON?

—ROCKET, *GUARDIANS OF THE GALAXY*

THANK YOU, SWEET RABBIT.

—THOR, *AVENGERS: INFINITY WAR*

NICK FURY: Do you know how to fly this thing?

CAROL DANVERS: We'll see. . . .

NICK FURY: Well, see, that's a yes-or-no question.

CAROL DANVERS: Yes.

NICK FURY: That's what I'm talking about!

—*CAPTAIN MARVEL*

I'VE BEEN FIGHTING WITH ONE ARM TIED BEHIND MY BACK, BUT WHAT HAPPENS WHEN I'M FINALLY SET FREE?

—CAPTAIN MARVEL, *CAPTAIN MARVEL*

CAROL DANVERS: What is it?

NICK FURY: It's the S.H.I.E.L.D. logo.

CAROL DANVERS: Does announcing your identity on clothing help with the covert part of your job?

NICK FURY: Said the space soldier who was wearing a rubber suit.

—*CAPTAIN MARVEL*

THOR: You'll pay for this!

VALKYRIE: No, I *got* paid for this.

—*THOR: RAGNAROK*

"You cannot talk!

One more word,

and I will feed you

to my children.

I'm kidding.

We are vegetarians."

—M'Baku, *Black Panther*

TAKE THE TESSERACT, LEAVE THE LUNCH BOX.

—CAPTAIN MARVEL, *CAPTAIN MARVEL*

[GOOSE,] I'M TRUSTING YOU NOT TO EAT ME.

—NICK FURY, *CAPTAIN MARVEL*

"There was one time when we were children, he transformed himself into a snake, and he knows that I love snakes. So I went to pick up the snake to admire it, and he transformed back into himself and he was like, 'Yeah, it's me!' And he stabbed me."

—Thor, *Thor: Ragnarok*

"Testing brand-new hero tech is dangerous, and you used to do that. You'd miss the coolest mission in the history of missions to stay here . . . ? I just think you should consider the example you're setting for your daughter."

—Monica Rambeau, *Captain Marvel*

YOUR MOM IS LUCKY. WHEN THEY WERE HANDING OUT KIDS, THEY GAVE HER THE TOUGHEST ONE. LIEUTENANT TROUBLE.

—CAROL DANVERS, *CAPTAIN MARVEL*

HULK . . . SMASH!

—HULK, *THE INCREDIBLE HULK*

"I like your plan,

except it sucks.

So let me do

the plan,

and that way,

it might be

really good."

—Star-Lord, *Avengers: Infinity War*

OD

TY.

—NICK FURY,
CAPTAIN MARVEL

"In my experience, no unmanned aerial vehicle will ever trump a pilot's instinct."

—James "Rhodey" Rhodes, *Iron Man*

I HAVE NOTHING TO PROVE TO YOU.

—CAPTAIN MARVEL, *CAPTAIN MARVEL*

KICK NAMES, TAKE ASS!

—MANTIS, *AVENGERS: INFINITY WAR*

"Language!"

—Captain America, *Avengers: Age of Ultron*

"I was meant

to be new.

I was meant

to be beautiful.

The world would've

looked to the sky

and seen hope . . .

seen mercy.

Instead they'll look up

in horror."

—Ultron, *Avengers: Age of Ultron*

WHY DON'T YOU PICK ON SOMEONE YOUR OWN SIZE?

—SCOTT LANG, *ANT-MAN*

STEPHEN STRANGE: Seriously?
You don't have any money?

WONG: Attachment to the material is detachment from the spiritual.

STEPHEN STRANGE: I'll tell the guys at the deli. Maybe they'll make you a metaphysical ham on rye.

—*AVENGERS: INFINITY WAR*

"Nothing goes over my head.

My reflexes are too fast.

I would catch it."

—Drax, *Guardians of the Galaxy*

SIF: I've got this completely under control!

THOR: Is that why everything's on fire?

SIR, I'M GOING TO HAVE TO ASK YOU TO EXIT THE DONUT.

—NICK FURY, *IRON MAN 2*

BLACK WIDOW: You do anything fun Saturday night?

CAPTAIN AMERICA: Well, all the guys from my barbershop
quartet are dead, so . . . no, not really.

—*CAPTAIN AMERICA: THE WINTER SOLDIER*

"Who's putting coffee grounds in the disposal? Am I running a bed-and-breakfast for a biker gang?"

—Tony Stark, *Captain America: Civil War*

...E BULLIES. ...T CARE ...Y'RE FROM.

—STEVE ROGERS, *CAPTAIN AMERICA: THE FIRST AVENGER*

DOCTOR STRANGE: I'm not ready.

THE ANCIENT ONE: No one ever is.

—*DOCTOR STRANGE*

I'M NOT GETTING DRAGGED INTO ANOTHER ONE OF ODIN'S FAMILY SQUABBLES.

—VALKYRIE, *THOR: RAGNAROK*

WE'RE IN THE ENDGAME NOW.

—DOCTOR STRANGE, *AVENGERS: INFINITY WAR*

"Today

  we don't

  fight for

  one life,

  we fight for

  all of them."

—Black Panther, *Avengers: Infinity War*

HULK: Huuullllkkkk!

THOR: Hey! We know each other! He's a friend from work.

—THOR: RAGNAROK

THIS CORSET IS REALLY UNCOMFORTABLE! SO COULD WE ALL JUST WRAP IT UP AND GO HOME?

—SHURI, *BLACK PANTHER*

I'M NOT REALLY WHO YOU THINK I AM.

—CAROL DANVERS, *CAPTAIN MARVEL*

"I'm just a kid from Brooklyn."

—Steve Rogers, *Captain America: The First Avenger*

WONG: We did it.

KARL MORDO: Yes. Yes, we did it.
By also violating the natural law.

DOCTOR STRANGE: Look around you. It's over.

KARL MORDO: You still think there will be no
consequences, Strange? No price to pay?
We broke our rules. . . . The bill comes
due. *Always* a reckoning.

—*DOCTOR STRANGE*

NICK FURY: We have no idea what other intergalactic threats are out there. And our one-woman security force had a prior commitment on the other side of the universe. S.H.I.E.L.D. alone can't protect us. We need more.

PHIL COULSON: More weapons?

NICK FURY: More *heroes.*

—*CAPTAIN MARVEL*

NICK FURY: YOU'RE A KREE. A RACE OF NOBLE WARRIORS?

VERS: HEROES. NOBLE WARRIOR HEROES.

—*CAPTAIN MARVEL*

M'BAKU: This will be the end of Wakanda.

OKOYE: Then it will be the noblest ending in history.

—*AVENGERS: INFINITY WAR*

PART OF THE
JOURNEY IS
THE END.

—TONY STARK, *AVENGERS: ENDGAME*

THE ENTIRE TIME I KNEW THANOS, HE
ONLY EVER HAD ONE GOAL: TO BRING
BALANCE TO THE UNIVERSE BY WIPING
OUT HALF OF ALL LIFE. HE USED TO KILL
PEOPLE PLANET BY PLANET, MASSACRE
BY MASSACRE. IF HE GETS ALL SIX
INFINITY STONES, HE CAN DO IT WITH
THE SNAP OF HIS FINGERS.

—GAMORA, *AVENGERS: INFINITY WAR*

"I know what

it's like to lose.

To feel so

desperately

that you're right.

Yet to fail

nonetheless . . .

Dread it.

Run from it.

Destiny arrives

all the same."

—Thanos, *Avengers: Infinity War*

"I know I'm asking a lot, but the price of freedom is high; it always has been. And it's a price I'm willing to pay. And if I'm the only one, then so be it. But I'm willing to bet I'm not."

—Steve Rogers, *Captain America: The Winter Soldier*

THE WORLD HAS CHANGED AND NONE OF US CAN GO BACK. ALL WE CAN DO IS OUR BEST, AND SOMETIMES THE BEST THAT WE CAN DO IS TO START OVER.

—PEGGY CARTER, *CAPTAIN AMERICA: THE WINTER SOLDIER*

I'M NOT GOING TO FIGHT YOUR WAR. I'M GOING TO END IT.

—CAPTAIN MARVEL, *CAPTAIN MARVEL*

RONAN: We'll be back for the weapon.

ACCUSER: The core?

RONAN: The woman.

—*CAPTAIN MARVEL*

To Marvel fans: We love you three thousand.

© 2019 MARVEL

All rights reserved. Published by Marvel Press, an imprint of Disney Book Group. No part of this book may be reproduced or transmitted in any form or by any means, electronic or mechanical, including photocopying, recording, or by any information storage and retrieval system, without written permission from the publisher. For information address Marvel Press, 125 West End Avenue, New York, New York 10023.

First Edition, September 2019
10 9 8 7 6 5 4 3 2 1
FAC-034274-19200
Printed in the United States of America

This book is set in Athelas and Avenir
Designed by Catalina Castro

Library of Congress Control Number: 2019937256
ISBN: 978-1-368-05381-5
Visit www.DisneyBooks.com
and www.Marvel.com

ANT-MAN
Directed by Peyton Reed
Screenplay by Edgar Wright & Joe Cornish and Adam McKay &
Paul Rudd
Story by Edgar Wright & Joe Cornish
Produced by Kevin Feige, p.g.a.
Executive Producers: Louis D'Esposito, Alan Fine, Victoria
Alonso, Michael Grillo, Stan Lee, and Edgar Wright
Co-Producers: Brad Winderbaum and David J. Grant
Associate Producer: Lars P. Winther

ANT-MAN AND THE WASP
Directed by Peyton Reed
Written by Chris McKenna & Erik Sommers and Paul Rudd &
Andrew Barrer & Gabriel Ferrari
Produced by Kevin Feige and Stephen Broussard
Executive Producers: Louis D'Esposito, Victoria Alonso, Charles
Newirth, and Stan Lee
Co-Producers: Mitch Bell and Lars P. Winther

THE AVENGERS
Directed by Joss Whedon
Screenplay by Joss Whedon
Story by Zak Penn and Joss Whedon
Produced by Kevin Feige
Executive Producers: Louis D'Esposito, Patricia Whitcher, Victoria
Alonso, Jeremy Latcham, Alan Fine, Jon Favreau, and Stan Lee

AVENGERS: AGE OF ULTRON
Written and directed by Joss Whedon
Produced by Kevin Feige, p.g.a.
Executive Producers: Louis D'Esposito, Alan Fine, Victoria
Alonso, Jeremy Latcham, Patricia Whitcher, Jon Favreau, and Stan
Lee
Co-Producer: Mitch Bell

AVENGERS: ENDGAME
Directed by Anthony and Joe Russo
Screenplay by Christopher Markus & Stephen McFeely
Produced by Kevin Feige
Executive Producers: Louis D'Esposito, Victoria Alonso, Michael
Grillo, Trinh Tran, Jon Favreau, James Gunn, and Stan Lee
Co-Producers: Mitch Bell, Christopher Markus, and Stephen
McFeely

AVENGERS: INFINITY WAR
Directed by Anthony and Joe Russo
Screenplay by Christopher Markus & Stephen McFeely
Produced by Kevin Feige, p.g.a.
Executive Producers: Louis D'Esposito, Victoria Alonso, Michael
Grillo, Trinh Tran, Jon Favreau, James Gunn, and Stan Lee
Co-Producer: Mitch Bell

BLACK PANTHER
Directed by Ryan Coogler
Written by Ryan Coogler & Joe Robert Cole
Produced by Kevin Feige, p.g.a.
Executive Producers: Louis D'Esposito, Victoria Alonso, Nate
Moore, Jeffrey Chernov, and Stan Lee
Co-Producer: David J. Grant

CAPTAIN AMERICA: CIVIL WAR
Directed by Anthony and Joe Russo
Screenplay by Christopher Markus & Stephen McFeely
Produced by Kevin Feige, p.g.a.
Executive Producers: Louis D'Esposito, Victoria Alonso, Patricia
Whitcher, Nate Moore, and Stan Lee
Co-Producer: Mitch Bell
Associate Producer: Lars P. Winther

CAPTAIN AMERICA: THE FIRST AVENGER
Directed by Joe Johnston
Screenplay by Christopher Markus & Stephen McFeely
Produced by Kevin Feige
Executive Producers: Louis D'Esposito, Joe Johnston, Nigel
Gostelow, Alan Fine, Stan Lee, and David Maisel
Co-Producers: Stephen Broussard and Victoria Alonso

CAPTAIN AMERICA: THE WINTER SOLDIER
Directed by Anthony and Joe Russo
Screenplay by Christopher Markus & Stephen McFeely
Produced by Kevin Feige, p.g.a.
Executive Producers: Louis D'Esposito, Alan Fine, Victoria Alonso,
Michael Grillo, and Stan Lee
Co-Producer: Nate Moore
Associate Producers: Mitch Bell and Lars P. Winther

CAPTAIN MARVEL
Directed by Anna Boden & Ryan Fleck
Screenplay by Anna Boden & Ryan Fleck & Geneva Robertson-Dworet

Story by Nicole Perlman & Meg Lefauve and Anna Boden &
Ryan Fleck & Geneva Robertson-Dworet
Produced by Kevin Feige
Executive Producers: Louis D'Esposito, Victoria Alonso,
Jonathan Schwartz, Patricia Whitcher, and Stan Lee
Co-Producer: David J. Grant and Lars P. Winther

DOCTOR STRANGE
Directed by Scott Derrickson
Written by Jon Spaihts and Scott Derrickson & C. Robert Cargill
Produced by Kevin Feige
Executive Producers: Louis D'Esposito, Victoria Alonso,
Stephen Broussard, Charles Newirth, and Stan Lee
Co-Producer: David J. Grant

GUARDIANS OF THE GALAXY
Directed by James Gunn
Screenplay by James Gunn and Nicole Perlman
Produced by Kevin Feige, p.g.a.
Executive Producers: Louis D'Esposito, Alan Fine, Victoria
Alonso, Jeremy Latcham, Nik Korda, and Stan Lee
Co-Producers: David J. Grant and Jonathan Schwartz

GUARDIANS OF THE GALAXY VOL. 2
Written and directed by James Gunn
Produced by Kevin Feige, p.g.a.
Executive Producers: Louis D'Esposito, Victoria Alonso,
Jonathan Schwartz, Nik Korda, and Stan Lee
Co-Producers: Lars P. Winther & David J. Grant
Associate Producer: Simon Hatt

THE INCREDIBLE HULK
Directed by Louis Leterrier
Screen Story and Screenplay by Zak Penn
Produced by Avi Arad, Gale Anne Hurd, and Kevin Feige
Executive Producers: Stan Lee, David Maisel, Jim Van Wyck
Associate Producer: Stephen Broussard

IRON MAN
Directed by Jon Favreau
Screenplay by Mark Fergus & Hawk Ostby and Art Marcum &
Matt Holloway
Produced by Avi Arad and Kevin Feige
Executive Producers: Denis L. Stewart, Louis D'Esposito, Jon
Favreau, Susan Downey, Alan Fine, Stan Lee, and David Maisel
Associate Producer: Jeremy Latcham

IRON MAN 2
Directed by Jon Favreau
Screenplay by Justin Theroux
Produced by Kevin Feige
Executive Producers: Alan Fine, Stan Lee, David Maisel, Denis
L. Stewart, Louis D'Esposito, Jon Favreau, and Susan Downey
Co-Producers: Jeremy Latcham and Victoria Alonso
Associate Producers: Karen Johnson and Eric N. Heffron

IRON MAN 3
Directed by Shane Black
Screenplay by Drew Pearce & Shane Black
Produced by Kevin Feige
Executive Producers: Jon Favreau, Louis D'Esposito, Charles
Newirth, Victoria Alonso, Stephen Broussard, Alan Fine, Stan
Lee, and Dan Mintz
Associate Producers: Lars P. Winther and Mitch Bell

THOR
Directed by Kenneth Branagh
Screenplay by Ashley Edward Miller & Zack Stentz and Don
Payne
Story by J. Michael Straczynski and Mark Protosevich
Produced by Kevin Feige
Executive Producers: Patricia Whitcher, Louis D'Esposito, Alan
Fine, Stan Lee, and David Maisel
Co-Producers: Craig Kyle and Victoria Alonso

THOR: THE DARK WORLD
Directed by Alan Taylor
Screenplay by Christopher L. Yost and Christopher Markus &
Stephen McFeely
Story by Don Payne and Robert Rodat
Produced by Kevin Feige, p.g.a.
Executive Producers: Louis D'Esposito, Victoria Alonso, Craig
Kyle, Alan Fine, Nigel Gostelow, and Stan Lee
Associate Producers: David J. Grant and Jamie Christopher

THOR: RAGNAROK
Directed by Taika Waititi
Written by Eric Pearson and Craig Kyle & Christopher L. Yost
Produced by Kevin Feige, p.g.a.
Executive Producers: Louis D'Esposito, Victoria Alonso, Brad
Winderbaum, Thomas M. Hammel, and Stan Lee
Co-Producer: David J. Grant

THE TRUTH IS A MATTER OF CIRCUMSTANCES. IT'S NOT ALL THINGS TO ALL PEOPLE ALL THE TIME, AND NEITHER AM I.

—BLACK WIDOW, *CAPTAIN AMERICA: THE WINTER SOLDIER*

I'M HOPING IF YOU P
CELEBRATION. I HOPE
I HOPE WE GET IT BACK
A NORMAL VERSION O
RESTORED . . . THIS TIM
WE'RE GOING TO TRY AN
IT'S GOT ME SCRATCHIN
SURVIVABILITY OF IT. T
HERO GIG. PART OF THE J
MADE THIS JOURNEY
GOING TO WORK OUT
SUPPOSED TO. **I LOVE Y**